Raise a Rain Forest

By William Anthony

Minneapolis, Minnesota

Credits

Cover – Svvell Design, derter, IconBunny, Alexandr Vorobev, Sorn340 Studio Images, David Jara Bogunya. 4–5 – Ardea-studio, avian, Kirasolly, Alex Oakenman, MaryDesy, worldclassphoto, BorneoRimbawan. 6–7 – Elena Paletskaya, Ksusha Dusmikeeva, GoodStudio, Jakob Weyde, Avigator Fortuner, szefei. 8–9 – Kirasolly, leungchopan, KarenHBlack, raditya. 10–11 – AustralianCamera, Sara Berdon, Chansom Pantip. 12–13 – BorneoRimbawan. 14–15 – POKPAK101, Kathryn L. Schipper, Uwe Bergwitz. 16–17 – Koshevnyk, barkarola, Andrew Krasovitckii, Vladimir Wrangel, outdoorsman, Kamran Karimov, funnybear36, Bildagentur Zoonar GmbH. 18–19 – NotionPic, Andrew Krasovitckii, Ondrej Prosicky, Ken Griffiths, Pesek Photo, Evgeniya Mokeeva, H.Elvin, Vectors Bang. 20–21 – olesia_g, Rich Carey, VikiVector, Halfpoint, Syda Productions, HappyPictures, Enric Adell Illustration. 22–23 – olnik_y, Virinaflora, SunshineVector.

Library of Congress Cataloging-in-Publication Data is available at www.loc.gov or upon request from the publisher.

ISBN: 978-1-63691-484-8 (hardcover)
ISBN: 978-1-63691-489-3 (paperback)
ISBN: 978-1-63691-494-7 (ebook)

© 2022 Booklife Publishing
This edition is published by arrangement with Booklife Publishing.

North American adaptations © 2022 Bearport Publishing Company. All rights reserved. No part of this publication may be reproduced in whole or in part, stored in a retrieval system, or transmitted in any form or by any means, electronic, mechanical, photocopying, recording, or otherwise, without written permission from the publisher.

For more information, write to Bearport Publishing, 5357 Penn Avenue South, Minneapolis, MN 55419. Printed in the United States of America.

Contents

How to Build Our World 4
Fit the Forest Floor 6
Add the Understory 8
Construct the Canopy 10
Build the Emergent Layer 12
Set Up the Weather 14
Invite the Animals 16
Add More Animals 18
Protect the Place 20
Make Your Own Environment . . . 22
Glossary 24
Index 24

How to Build Our World

Our world is amazing. It is full of places to go and things to see. There are different **environments**, from rain forests to cities. Each one has plants, animals, and more.

What does a rain forest environment look like? Let's build one to find out!

Fit the Forest Floor

Rain forests have four different layers. We'll start on the ground with the lowest layer, which is called the forest floor. Lots of things live down there.

Bugs and **fungi** live on the forest floor. They break down dead plants and animals.

Only a tiny bit of sunlight reaches the forest floor.

Rivers are part of the forest floor. Many animals live in or near the rivers.

Add the Understory

Let's start building upward! The layer above the forest floor is called the understory.

The understory layer has small trees and **shrubs**.

Many of these plants grow bright, colorful flowers.

Some grow fruit that become food for animals.

Construct the Canopy

Next, we'll add a layer of treetops above the understory. This is called the canopy.

The treetops that make up the canopy are very close together. They are like a big, leafy roof for the rain forest.

The canopy blocks out lots of sunshine. This is why the forest floor does not have much light.

The canopy is full of fruits and nuts that grow on trees all year.

Build the Emergent Layer

The last layer we need to add to our rain forest is the emergent layer. It's at the very top!

The tallest trees in the rain forest make up the emergent layer. These trees can be up to 230 feet (70 m) tall.

Set Up the Weather

We know the top layer can get sunny and windy, but what's the weather like for the whole rain forest? Let's set it up . . .

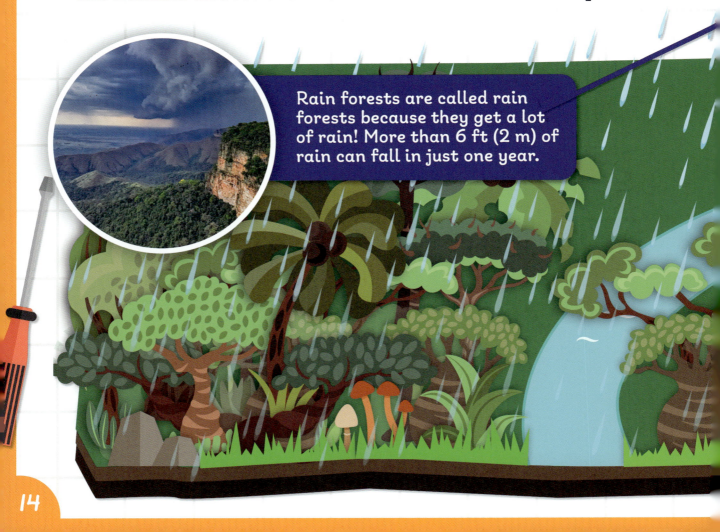

Rain forests are called rain forests because they get a lot of rain! More than 6 ft (2 m) of rain can fall in just one year.

Invite the Animals

Now that we've got our four layers set up, it's time to add animals! Although there aren't many rain forests, more than half of the world's animal and plant **species** live in these places.

The forest floor has many bugs. Other animals, such as anteaters, eat the bugs!

Crocodiles, jaguars, and other animals swim in rain forest rivers.

Many animals live in the small understory trees. Some snakes and frogs can climb into trees! Bats fly nearby.

17

Add More Animals

There are even more animals in the treetops! They are very different from the animals near the ground.

The emergent layer is home to lots of birds. Scarlet macaws live among the tallest trees.

The tallest tree branches may break easily. That's why some animals, such as feathertail gliders, move between trees by **gliding** instead of climbing.

Monkeys climb through the trees. Sloths and many other animals do, too.

Protect the Place

Rain forests are full of life! And all the plants and animals in these environments are very important to our planet. However, humans are harming rain forests.

People are cutting down trees. This destroys the homes of many animals.

But there are ways we can help. We can plant new trees.

Some trees are used to make paper. If we **recycle** paper, we do not have to cut down as many trees.

Make Your Own Environment

Rain forest environments are incredible! They have awesome animals, tall trees, and pretty plants. Now, it's time to build your own environment! You could draw it, paint it, or write about it. What do you want to put in your rain forest?

What will the weather be like in your rain forest?

What will your plants and trees look like?

Which animals will live in your environment?

Glossary

environments the different parts of our world in which people, animals, and plants live

equator the imaginary line around Earth that is an equal distance from the North and South Poles

fungi living things that look like plants but have no flowers

gliding flying or moving smoothly through the air without effort

recycle to use something again by making it into something new

shrubs types of small plants

species groups that animals are divided into, according to things they have in common

Index

animals 4, 6–7, 9, 16–20, 22–23
equator 15
flowers 9
fruit 9, 11
light 7, 11, 13
rain 14–15
recycle 21
shrubs 8–9
sun 7, 11, 13–14
trees 8, 10–13, 15, 17–23